05. 01.
10. 05.

11. 15.   05. 04.
11. 03.

05. 09.

06. 04.
11. 12.

07. 03.
12. 05.

07. 09.

03. 10.
14. 05.

09. 02.

09. 06.

09. 11.

BG

Rhif/No. 26547112   Dosb./Class ___ YF

Dylid dychwelyd neu adnewyddu'r eitem erbyn neu cyn y dyddiad a nodir uchod.
Oni wneir hyn gellir codi tal.

This book is to be returned or renewed on or before the last date stamped above,
otherwise a charge may be made.

LLT1

Also by Michael Morpurgo

MORE
MUCK AND MAGIC

Edited by

MICHAEL MORPURGO

Illustrated by

QUENTIN BLAKE

Foreword by HRH The Princess Royal

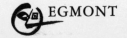
EGMONT

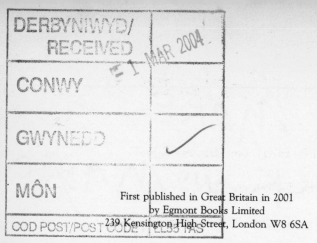
First published in Great Britain in 2001
by Egmont Books Limited
239 Kensington High Street, London W8 6SA

Compilation © 2001 Michael Morpurgo

The Cow, Worms, The Fox, Swallows and Badger from *What Is The Truth*
by Ted Hughes published by Faber and Faber Ltd
'What's the Country?' © 2001 Jacqueline Wilson
Winter on the Moon © 2001 Sam McBratney
The Princess of Strawberryland © 2001 Joan Aiken Enterprises
The Tree Rider of Izanda © 2001 Margaret Mahy
It's a Dog's Life © 2001 Michael Morpurgo
Brook Dancer © 2001 Gillian Cross
The Hen and Bull Story © 2001 Jan Mark
Mona © 2001 Jamila Gavin

Illustrations © 2001 Quentin Blake

The moral rights of the editor, authors and illustrators have been asserted

ISBN 0 7497 4094 9

10 9 8 7 6 5 4 3 2

A CIP catalogue record for this title is available from the British Library

Printed and bound in Great Britain by Cox & Wyman Ltd, Reading,
Berkshire

Contents

This book is dedicated to all those good and kind people who have helped Farms for City Children through its first 25 years.

To HRH The Princess Royal, our Patron. To the late Poet Laureate Ted Hughes, our founding President. To Quentin Blake, the first Children's Laureate, and one of our Vice-Presidents.

To all the authors, illustrators, publishers, farmers, friends, staff and benefactors whose great generosity has sustained and supported us throughout.

And last, but certainly not least, to the many thousands of city children and their teachers who have been farmers for a week at Nethercott, or Treginnis or Wick, over these last years.

Clare and Michael Morpurgo

www.farmsforcitychildren.co.uk

In the last 25 years some 40,000 children from our towns and cities have had the chance to spend a week down on the farm - either at Nethercott in Devon, where Farms for City Children began, or at Treginnis Isaf on the coast of Pembrokeshire, or at Wick Court in Gloucestershire.

All three farms are different - Nethercott a mixed dairy, sheep and arable farm along the banks of the River Torridge, Treginnis Isaf a hill farm by the sea with 1000 breeding ewes where the seals come to have their pups on the beaches and Wick Court an organic farm where they make Double Gloucester cheese from the milk of Gloucester cows, where Gloucester pigs wander at will.

But the farms have one thing in common; each farm welcomes about 1000 children every year. They come with their teachers and effectively become farmers for a week. Because they are really involved with the running of the farm, they see for themselves the reality of life in the countryside - its beauty and its harshness, all the joys and discomforts.

They find out where their food comes from and what it takes to grow it. They make hay in the heat, they feed the sheep in the snow. Within the bounds of safety they join in all they can.

But it is not all work . There is time to play in the fields and to go on long muddy walks, and a time each evening to settle down in front of the fire for a story, maybe one of these. I hope so.

Anne

The Cow
by
Ted Hughes

The Cow is but a bagpipe,
All bag, all bones, all blort.
They bawl me out of bed at dawn
And never give a thought
               a thought
They never give a thought.

The milk-herd is a factory:
Milk, meat, butter, cheese.
You think these come in rivers? O
The slurry comes in seas
               seas
The slurry comes in seas.

The Cow

A cowclap is an honest job,

A black meringue for the flies.

But when the sea of slurry spills

Your shining river dies

                dies

Your shining river dies.

Say this about cows:

Nothing can stop

From one end the Moo

From t'other the flop

             flop

             flop

             flippety-flop

Floppety-flippety.

"What's the Country?"
by
Jacqueline Wilson

'Mick's coming round on Saturday,' said Mum.

Skippy smiled. She always smiles. If you told her the Bogeyman was coming to take her out to tea she'd clap her hands and smile.

I didn't smile. I can't stick Mick. I don't see why Mum has to have a stupid boyfriend at her age. She says he makes her happy. I can't see why she can't just be happy with Skippy and me.

'Mick's going to take us on a special day

out!' Mum announced.

Skippy smiled. I very nearly smiled too. We didn't often get special days out.

I wondered where we might be going. A day trip to Disneyland? No, maybe not. But maybe Mick would take us to the Red River Theme Park and we could go on all the really brilliant rides where you swoop up and down and it's like you're flying right up in the sky.

'Will he take us to the Red River Theme Park, Mum?'

'Don't be daft, Hayley,' said Mum. 'It costs a fortune. Mick's not made of money. No, we're going to have a lovely day out in the country.'

'The *country?*' I said.

'What's the country?' Skippy asked.

'It's boring,' I said.

I hadn't actually been to the country much

but of course I knew all about it. We've got this old video about kids living on a farm in the country. The main girl in it is called Hayley like me. It's a good film but the country looks *awful*. Cold and empty and muddy, with cows that chase you.

I moaned and Mum said I was a spoilt little whatsit and I went into our bedroom and sulked. Skippy came and cuddled up beside me.

'We don't like the country,' she said, to show me she was on my side – though Skippy is always on *everyone's* side.

'That's right, Skip. We don't like the country. And we don't like Mick.'

'We don't like Mick,' Skippy echoed obediently, but she didn't sound so sure.

When Mick knocked at our door at nine o'clock on Saturday morning Skippy went rushing up to him going 'Mick, Mick, Mick!'

Skippy is useless at not liking people.

I am brilliant at it. And Mick was making it easy-peasy. He looked *ridiculous*. He always looks a bit wet and weedy but today he was wearing a big woolly jumper right up to his chin and awful baggy cord trousers and *boots*. Honestly. I knew Mum could act a bit loopy at times but she had to be barking mad to go round with Mick.

'Ready, girls?' he said, swinging Skippy round and round while she squealed and kicked her legs, her shoes falling off. 'Have you got any welly boots, Skip? I think you'll need them.' He put on a silly voice (well, his *own* voice is silly, but this was sillier). 'It gets right mucky in the country, lass.'

Skippy put on my old Kermit wellies and her Minnie Mouse mac.

'It's a mouse-frog!' said Mick, and Skippy

fell about laughing.

I sighed heavily.

'What about your wellies, Hayley?' said Mick. 'And I should put a jumper on too.'

I took no notice. As if I'd be seen dead in wellies! And I was wearing the simply incredible designer tee-shirt Mum found for 20p down at the school jumble. I wasn't going to cover it up with an old sweater even if it *snowed*.

Mum looked like she wanted to give me a shake, but she got distracted looking for our old thermos flask. We were having a picnic. I'd helped cut the sandwiches. (Skippy sucked the cut-off crusts until they went all slimy like ice lollies.) The sandwiches were egg and banana and ham (not all together though maybe it would taste good?) and there were apples and crisps and a giant bar of chocolate and orange juice for Skip and me and tea for Mum and Mick. It seemed a seriously yummy picnic. It looked like I *might* be going to enjoy this day out in spite of myself.

Skippy and I nagged to nibble the chocolate in the car on the way to the country. Mum said we had to wait till picnic time. Hours and hours and hours! Mick said 'Oh, let the girls have a piece now if they're really hungry.'

He rooted in the picnic bag and handed the whole bar over. This was a serious mistake. Skippy and I tucked in determinedly. By the time Mum peered round at us we'd eaten nearly three-quarters.

Mum was very cross.

'How can you be so greedy? Hayley, you should have stopped Skippy. You know she gets car sick.'

'She's fine, Mum. Stop fussing. You're OK, aren't you, Skip? You don't feel sick, do you?'

Skippy said she didn't feel sick at all. She tried to smile. She was very pale, though her lips were dark brown with chocolate.

'Oh dear,' said Mum. 'Have you got a spare plastic bag, Mick? We need it kind of urgently.'

She was just in time. Skippy was very very sick. It was so revolting that it made *me* feel a little bit sick too. We drove slowly with the window wide open. I shut my eyes and wondered when we were ever going to get to this boring old countryside. I'd lost interest in the picnic. I just wanted it to be time to go home.

'Here we are!' Mick said cheerily at long long long last.

I opened my eyes and looked around. I

hadn't realised the country was going to be so *green*. That old film with the other Hayley was in black and white.

'We used to come here on days out when I was a boy,' Mick said excitedly. 'Isn't it lovely?'

There was nothing much *there*. No shops. No cafés. Not even an ice-cream van. Just lots and lots of trees. And fields. More trees. More fields. And a big big hill in the distance, so tall there were grey clouds all round the top like fuzzy hair.

'That's Lookout Hill,' said Mick. 'Right, girls! Let's climb it!'

I stared at him as if he was mad. Even Mum looked taken aback. He said it as if climbing miles up into the clouds was a big treat! We don't reckon it so great climbing three flights of stairs up to our flat when the lift breaks down.

'Isn't it a bit too far?' said Mum.

'No, no. We'll be up it in a matter of minutes, you'll see,' said Mick.

Mick is a liar. Those few minutes went on for hours. First we trudged through the woods. It was freezing cold and dark and miserable and I hated it. Mick saw me shivering and offered me his big woolly but I wouldn't wear it. He put it on Skip instead, right over her mac. She staggered along looking loopy, the hem right down round her ankles. Mum said she looked like a little sheep so Skip went baa baa baa.

Then we were out of the wood and walking across a field. Skip went skipping about until she stepped in something disgusting. I laughed at her. Then I stepped in something too. I squealed and moaned and wiped my shoes five hundred times in the grass. We seemed to be wading through a vast animal toilet.

'Stop making such a fuss, Hayley. We'll clean your shoes properly when we get home,' said Mum.

She didn't look as if she was enjoying the country that much either. Her hair was blowing all over the place and her eye make-up was running.

'Now for the final stretch,' said Mick, taking Mum's hand. She held on to Skippy with the other.

I hung back. I climbed up after them. Up and up and up and up. And up and up and up. And up some more.

My head hurt and my chest was tight and a stitch stabbed my side and my legs ached so much I couldn't keep up.

'This sucks,' I gasped, and I sat down hard on the damp mucky grass.

'Come on, Hayley!' Mick called, holding out his other hand.

'No thanks. I'll wait here. I don't want to go up the stupid hill,' I said.

'You've got to come too, Hayley,' said Mum. 'We can't leave you here by yourself.'

So they forced me up and I had to stagger onwards. Up and up and up and up. I wasn't cold any more. I was boiling hot. My designer tee-shirt was sticking to me. My shoes were not only all mucky and spoilt, but they were giving me blisters. If I was as little as Skippy I might have started crying.

'It'll be worth it when we get right to the top and you see the view,' said Mick.

What view? He was crazy. We were right

up in the clouds and it was grey and gloomy and drizzling.

'Nearly there!' Mad Mick yelled above me. 'See!'

Then Mum gasped. Skippy squeaked. And I staggered up after them out of the clouds – and there I was on the top of the hill and the sun was suddenly out, shining just for us right above the clouds in this private secret world in the air. There were real sheep munching grass and a Skippy-sheep capering around like crazy. I stood still, my heart thumping, the breeze cool on my hot cheeks, looking up at the vast sky. I saw a bird flying way up even higher. I felt as if I could fly too. Just one more step and I'd be soaring.

The clouds below were drifting and parting and suddenly I could see the view. I could see for miles and miles and miles – the green slopes and the dark woods and the silver river glittering in the sunlight. I was on top of the whole world!

'Wow!' I said.

Skippy smiled. Mum smiled. Mick smiled. And I smiled too. Then we all ran hand in hand down down down the hill, ready for our picnic.

Winter on the Moon
by
Sam McBratney

Long ago, people had no idea where migratory birds went during the winter. It was quite common for people to believe that the birds lived at the bottom of a pond, or flew off to the moon.

He was one of nine fluffy chicks lying in the snug and warm, and his home was in the long grass.

Two days after hatching out he stood up on wobbly legs and fell from the nest. Luckily for him corncrakes build their nests on the ground, so he didn't have far to fall. His mother Greywing called him Rascal because of all the trouble he gave her.

Rascal loved to wander away on his own to look for slugs at the edge of the hay meadow. One morning as he tried to catch a butterfly that had given him the slip once or twice, he heard a noise in the distance. A rushing wind whipped through the grass; and frogs and mice, with other animals of the fields, fled in terror from the coming din.

His mother Greywing had often told him about the Moving Noise – it was what corncrakes feared most of all. And it was coming now. Rascal put down his head and ran towards the safest place he knew.

But the nest in the long grass had disappeared, along with Greywing and his brothers and sisters. Rascal blinked to shut out the light as the Moving Noise turned towards him once again.

'Get out of there,' a voice called out, 'or it'll finish you, too!'

This was a dark bird whom Rascal had often seen in the alder trees. Rascal fluttered after him into the nearest hedge, where they sat for some time, looking out over the mown field. The long grass was all gone.

The dark bird spoke first. 'Are you all right? You corncrakes are funny birds. Why build your nest in the middle of a field, of all places? Still, I suppose it takes all sorts.'

But Rascal, remembering only the fun of tumbling in and out of the tangled nest in the hay meadow, made no reply to that.

Then he said, 'Will I ever see them again?'

'No. I'll help you as best I can, young fella, but you're on your own now and that's just the way it is. Foggy's the name, by the way – they call me Foggy.'

In the summer weeks that followed, Rascal learned that he must try not to think of how he had lost Greywing. He caught crane-flies under the trees and took snails among the rushes near the lake. While feeding in the early morning he often met up with Foggy, who usually had some advice to give him.

'Watch out for overhead wires,' Foggy would say. 'And magpies! Believe me, those boys will do you no favours.'

Towards the end of summer when the

days grew shorter and the nights grew colder, Rascal came to say goodbye to Foggy.

'I have to make the Journey,' he said. 'I'm not sure where to, but Greywing used to talk about it. I must fly to a place far away from here.'

Foggy had a lot to say about the Journey. 'Oh yes, I know all about *that*, your sort fly off for the winter. Funny birds, you corncrakes – can't stand a bit of ice and snow.'

'But where to?' asked Rascal.

'Well . . .' said Foggy, who didn't actually *know* where to, 'you're like swallows, aren't you? Swallows, willow-warblers, corncrakes, I've heard you all fly off to the moon, then come back again in the spring. Maybe I'll see you then,' Foggy called out as Rascal flew off.

But he didn't really believe that he would see Rascal again. Foggy had heard terrible stories about the Journey. There would be storms over the ocean. Many birds would fly into shining lights that swept through the darkness and never be seen again. They would fly over deserts where nothing grew and hunters would shoot them out of the sky with guns. What a business, thought Foggy, to prefer all that to a little snow!

The winter passed.

A soft rain fell in April as old Foggy looked down at the water in the ditch below. The whole world just then was full of puddles and drips. One drip landed on his beak as if someone up there was aiming at him.

All of a sudden he heard a voice close by that made him cheer up a bit. By Jove, he thought, there's a voice I know! That bird from last year – Rascal – was sitting as large as life two branches above him.

Foggy hopped over for some conversation. It had been a tough winter, not much company. Not much grub, either.

'You made it, then?' he said.

'I made it. And back again,' came the reply.

'And how was it? We've had snow and blasted gales here, you know. So tell me – what was the Journey like? How was winter on the moon?'

Rascal looked around him, thinking about the Journey he had just made. He hadn't been anywhere near the moon – it was impossible

for a bird to fly to the moon.

He had flown south for the winter, to Africa. And in the spring he had flown the hundreds of miles back again to be in this place where the grass was growing so well. It was time to make this his territory, a time for nest-building and rearing the young ones; a time to keep them as safe as possible from the fox and the hawk and the Moving Noise so that they too would grow up and make the Journey to poor old Foggy's moon.

This had been the way of his mother Greywing, and it would be his way – the way of the corncrake.

Worms
by
Ted Hughes

I hear for every acre there's a ton of
worms beneath.

I hear that worm-meat's better meat
than fatted barley beef.

We're farming only half our farms,
and that's the new belief.

I think I'm growing barley, bullocks,
pigs and lambs galore.

From six a.m. till nine at night I toil
my body sore.

But I'm only feeding the roots of the
worms, it's worms I'm working for.

Below my clover meadows worms are
   bellowing in the dark.
They're bound for nobody's oven,
   one or two might go to the lark.
They gobble their way through the
   earth's black pudding safe as they
   were in the ark.

Worms riot and revel in their rude
   and naked hordes.
And most of what I fatten, far, far
   more than my farm affords
Falls into their idle mouths, and the
   whole lot live like lords.

The Princess of Strawberryland

by
Joan Aiken

Strawberryland is a small country that lies among the mountains. Beyond its northern boundary lies Snogronia, icy cold and dark all day for six months of the year; and Sandischia, which is nothing but desert, lies to the south. But Strawberryland is warm and fertile, and its best crop, all the year round, is strawberries, which grow in the valleys as big as tennis balls; and even on the mountain slopes the wild strawberries are as large as marbles and have a most delicious flavour. Twice a year the strawberries are harvested and taken away on ships to other lands where people pay huge prices for them.

Nobody lives in Sandischia, for nothing will grow there. And the natives of Snogronia, who lead a very gloomy life, mostly in the dark, are eaten up with envy of their happy neighbours over the mountains, and so are always looking for an excuse to go to war.

One time it happened that the king of Strawberryland had gone to visit his sister, the queen of Sylvana, a country that lay far to the south. While he was absent the king left his country under the care of his daughter Euphrasia, who was only seventeen but very sensible.

'If there should be any trouble, just send a dove and I'll come back,' he said. 'But I don't think there will be any trouble.' And off he went, travelling by camel-caravan slowly across the desert.

Well, why should there be any trouble? thought Euphrasia. The winter strawberry crop is ready to pick. Everybody will be busy doing that.

The strawberries were scarlet and shining under their leaves in the fields. Even the air smelt sweet and fragrant. Euphrasia felt sorry for her father having to travel so far across the dry desert.

She went out into her own garden and picked some of her own strawberries, which were sweet and ripe and better than any other fruit in the whole world.

'Good morning, Princess!' said a voice over the garden wall. 'I have just found a crown in a cave. So I thought I had better bring it to you.'

The fair-haired young man who was

smiling at Euphrasia over the wall was Sam the shepherd who looked after the king's sheep, high up on the mountainsides, where the grass was thin, and it was too cold even for wild strawberries to grow.

'My goodness!' said Euphrasia, taking the crown from him. 'This looks very, very old.'

'I found it a long way back in a deep cave,' agreed Sam. 'I was hunting for a lamb that had gone astray. I expect it once belonged to one of the Old Old People who lived in this land before us.'

The crown was made of very thin, fine silver, beaten into a flat plate and curved round, with six points sticking up, and it had a raised design of strawberries and strawberry leaves and strawberry flowers. It was black and dirty and dusty from having lain underground for so long.

'I shall clean it and polish it,' said Euphrasia, 'and then I shall wear it at the Strawberry Fair.'

Twice a year in Strawberryland they hold harvest fairs, a summer fair and a winter fair, with a lot of music and dancing, to celebrate the end of each strawberry season, when all (or at least some) of the strawberries are sold to the foreign merchants who come in ships to the port of Strawberry Haven.

Euphrasia gently tried the thin old crown on her head and, for one startled moment, she thought she heard all the things that the birds were saying to each other overhead, and the mice under the pansy leaves, and the worms under the earth.

'The crown fits you very well, Princess,' said Sam the shepherd. 'Perhaps it is a magic crown and will give you three wishes. My

mother always used to say that the Old People, who lived here thousands of years before us, were cousins of the Sea People, and the Wind People, and had all kinds of powers and knowledge that we don't have any more.'

'Well,' said Princess Euphrasia, 'when I have cleaned and polished the crown, so that it looks as it did when it was new, I will put it on and then we shall see what it can do.'

So, every evening when she had finished her princess's work for the day, hearing petitions, and sorting out people's troubles, and visiting schools and hospitals, and entertaining foreign royalties, she sat herself down on the front steps of the palace and rubbed away at the crown with the tops of old cotton stockings which had been dipped in milk and hartshorn powder. Then she polished the crown hard with spirits of wine and arrowroot. And finally she brushed it with a thick soft brush made from fur that she had combed out of the palace cat.

After she had been doing this for about two weeks the silver crown began to shine and glow with a beautiful deep silvery shine.

Euphrasia was just thinking, one evening, that she would take the crown indoors and try it on in front of the throne-room mirror, and see what it looked like, when Sam the shepherd came rushing through the garden. He looked worried to death.

'Princess! Princess! Something terrible is happening! The Snogronians are invading our country!'

If this was true, it was most serious news. Every hundred years or so the Snogronians, fed up with their dismal dark freezing territory, and bitterly envious of their happy neighbours, would come pouring, in huge armies, over the frontier to the north, and try to grab the next-door country. They had done it in the time of Euphrasia's grandfather, and in the time of her great-great-grandfather, and both times there had been dreadful battles, and many people killed on both sides, before the Snow People were driven back to their own bleak land again.

'Oh good heavens!' said Euphrasia. 'Is that really happening? And Father so far away in Sylvana! Oh, how terrible!'

'Come and see for yourself,' said Sam the shepherd.

He led Euphrasia round to the back of the palace. From there, it was possible to see far away to the most distant mountains of the north, which were all covered with snow. And there, even without a telescope, Euphrasia could see massive armies all in motion, hordes of foot soldiers, and horsemen, and archers, and chariots, all creeping south down the mountainsides. They looked like armies of ants, they looked as if they were moving slowly, but in fact, as Euphrasia could see, they were coming very fast indeed.

'Oh my goodness, Sam! When do you think they will be here?'

'Tomorrow, at the very latest,' said Sam, peering between his fingers. 'Perhaps tonight.'

'I must send a dove off to Father! But even so, it will take a day to reach him, and it will take him three days to get back. And, anyway, what can he do? They are after our strawberries, and all our soldiers are hard at work picking the southern-most crop. What *ever* can we do?'

'Well,' said Sam, 'it's only a thought, but

how about putting on that crown that you have polished up so bright and shiny? One thing I do know about the Old People, they kept this land safe from trouble for hundreds of years. If that is an Old People's crown, perhaps it can help.'

So Euphrasia put the crown on her head. It fitted well and looked dazzlingly bright against her dark hair.

At once she heard what the moles were

saying to each other, under the ground.

'Hark at the thundering tread of those Snow People,' said one mole to another mole. 'They are trampling all over the burrows of our cousins up in the mountains. They will do a shocking lot of damage when they get here, with their heavy battle-horses and their copper-wheeled chariots and the soldiers all in boots with iron studs on. If only that girl, that princess, had any sense, she would call the

ghosts of the Old People to come back and
stand side by side in their old roads and fields
to stop the snow soldiers from stamping all
over this land, or at least to slow them down
until help can arrive.'

'*What* help?' said the other mole sadly. 'I
can feel in my black whiskers and in my broad
shovel-feet that there are hundreds and
thousands of those terrible people all coming
over the mountains. Who can possibly stop
them?'

But Euphrasia, clasping the crown on her
head with both hands, cried aloud:

'Old People! Old People! Can you hear
me? Will you come and help me? I am your
great-great-great-great-granddaughter
Euphrasia. I – and all your other great-great-
great-grandchildren – are in dreadful danger
from the Snow People. Come back, come

back, out of your caves and your graves, out of the deep sea, out of the deep forest, come back and help us now!'

Euphrasia did not cry in vain. Her voice went echoing through the streets of the town, and across the strawberry fields, and up the mountain sides, through the valleys and the caves and the forests and along the beaches. And the ghosts of the Old People, all, all the people who, for hundreds and hundreds, for thousands and thousands of years had ever lived in that land, making their hammers out of stone, making their houses out of sticks and skins, and then their descendants, who had tamed horses and tilled fields and had made wheeled carts, and houses of wood, and then castles of rock, had smelted metals and made jewels and written books and composed songs – all those ghosts came drifting from the ground, from the sea, from the forest, from the mountain caves. Thin and wispy they were, like smoke, like mist, and yet there were so many of them, so tremendously many, from times before even memory began, that the whole land was packed with ghosts, and you could feel them like a softness on the ground. Like a thickness in the air, so that it was hard to breathe, and even harder to move. People went staggering into their houses, feeling faint, feeling very queer, as if they had bumped into a solid wall of cloud.

As for the invading armies, they trudged

on, but more and more slowly. They could hardly push a passage through the immense mass of ghosts that hung and drifted and floated in their way. They came to the strawberry fields in the valleys, and they trampled carelessly over the shining, juicy crop, but the ghosts were so thick around them that they could not even stoop down to pick the berries, although they felt parched with thirst. The fruit were mashed into a red paste and the boots of the marching soldiers, the wheels of their waggons, the hoofs of their horses, were all stained scarlet. They staggered

and tottered, it was impossible to breathe, yet they came on.

If only we had some archers, thought Euphrasia, we could shoot them down.

But the archers were all hard at work picking fruit in the fields by the sea.

Then Euphrasia listened to what the silver crown had to tell her. She heard the voices of swallows, swooping and twittering round the palace eaves.

'If that girl, the princess, had any sense, she would send for the bees who are swarming over there to the east in Cherryland. The bees would soon send those Snow Folk back to their own place.'

Euphrasia didn't waste any time. Holding the silver crown tightly on her head, she cried as loud as she could:

'Bees! Bees! Oh, please! Dear bees, will

you come to Strawberryland, where we have a terrible infestation of Snow People?'

Then she waited.

'We had better go into your palace,' suggested Sam the shepherd. 'The bees may not know the difference between Snow People and Strawberry People.'

'What about your sheep?'

'Bees never sting sheep.'

So Euphrasia and Sam went into the palace, pushing their way with difficulty through many thicknesses of ghosts. It was like walking through shredded wheat. Luckily all the other Strawberry People had tottered into their homes too, struggling through layers of ghosts, because they hoped it might be easier to breathe indoors. And also they wanted to hide their most precious possessions before the Snow People arrived.

But the Snow People never did arrive.

Far to the east, along the tops of the mountains, which were not so high in that direction, a thin black line began to appear, stretching all the way from north to south. Gradually it became a thick black line. Then it became a cloud. Then the whole sky was black and buzzing with bees. Not just common bees, either. These were Giant Killer Bees. One sting would do for an elephant. They sank down like a dreadful blanket over the armies of the Snow People. They stung, they buzzed, they stung.

A wild wailing went up from the Snow Army. The people turned to run back, but there were hundreds more behind them and no way of escape. And, in front, the crowding ghosts blocked the way. Bees overhead and ghosts in front. What could they do? They fell to the ground and died among the strawberries.

The huge swarms of bees moved north over the snowy mountains. The warmth from their busy wings was enough to melt the snow on the slopes, and torrents of melted snow-water began to run down the slopes and the hillsides. This great flood washed the dead Snow People out to sea. The ones that were not stung to death or washed away were so terrified at what was happening to their mates that they turned round, pushed their way through the ghosts, and fled back the way they had come, disappearing into the northern mountains again. The bees had gone ahead of them, over the land of Snogronia, where they stung anyone who was so foolish as to stay out-of-doors, and on they flew, into the blossoming land of Appleheim, which has no human inhabitants, only reindeer. What became of the bees after that, who can say?

But Princess Euphrasia came out of her palace and looked anxiously about her. All the strawberry crop was washed away, along with the bodies of the invaders who had hoped to steal it.

But – as against that – not a single inhabitant of Strawberryland was killed or even wounded – except for half a dozen who were suffering from bee-stings.

'And the strawberries will grow again next year,' said Sam the shepherd.

'But now we have to get rid of these ghosts,' said Euphrasia.

For the ghosts were still everywhere, thick and heavy in the atmosphere like the smell of burnt toast. If you looked along the street, all the houses seemed pale and white and flaky, as if they were crumbling away, because of the layers of ghosts.

People grumbled that they couldn't start their cars, or ride their bicycles, or even shut their doors and windows, because of all the mass of ghosts that hung and hovered and dangled in the way.

So Princess Euphrasia, holding the silver crown very tightly on her head with both hands, called aloud to the ghosts:

'Dear ghosts! Thank you for coming to our help so speedily. We are everlastingly grateful to you. We hope we shall not need to trouble you again for hundreds of years. But now we expect that you are tired and would like to go back to your caves and graves and crannies and chasms and grottoes. However we are going to hold a Festival of Ghosts now, instead of our Winter Strawberry Fair, so, if any of you – perhaps the most recent ones – would prefer to stay for it, you are very kindly welcome.'

There was no need to wash away the mess of squashed strawberries, for the flood had done that, pouring along the streets of Strawberry Town. So in their clean and shining streets the Strawberry People danced and sang and rejoiced with their princess among them, wearing her silver crown. The festivities went on for three whole days and quite a number of ghosts took part at the start, but by the end of the third day even the liveliest and youngest ghost was glad to flap off and stow itself away in its cavern.

And people started preparing the strawberry beds for the next crop.

A week later, the king arrived home.

He was very astonished to see the fields

empty and bare, instead of covered with fruit and everybody hard at work picking. But when he heard the story of what had happened, and was shown the ancient silver crown, he said that his daughter Euphrasia had done very well, very well indeed, had rescued the land from terrible danger.

'I have read about this crown in old history books,' he said. 'It was made by my great-to-the-tenth-power grandfather who, as well as being king, was a wizard and a skilled silversmith. The crown has the power to grant three wishes to whomever it fits.'

'Well, I have had three wishes from it,' said Euphrasia. 'So my fourth wish will have to be granted without the help of the crown.'

'What is your fourth wish?' said the king.

Euphrasia said: 'I wish to marry Sam the shepherd.'

The Tree Rider of Izanda
by
Margaret Mahy

'I'm going to ride my horse,' said Bella. 'And while I ride it I'm going to sing.'

'Huh!' said Hamish. 'You can't sing!'

'Huh!' said Sharon. 'Everyone knows you haven't got a horse.'

But Bella left them behind and made for the grassy track that led to Halliday's Hill. 'Izanda!' she muttered. 'No more Halliday's Hill! Now you are the mysterious land of Izanda.'

The summery track tied Izanda to the mainland as if it were a wild horse held by a bridle of gold. Bella scrambled onward and upward until she came to the slope where black castles rose out of the long grass.

Long ago Izanda had been covered in forest . . . an ancient forest that got in the way of men wanting to farm, so those early farmers had set fire raging over the hills. Bella imagined the trees burning – tortured arms flung high, flames leaping up through their green hair. Their great charred stumps had become the blackened castles of Izanda.

Even though its forest was gone no one farmed Halliday's Hill these days, because there were no springs or streams to water sheep and cattle who needed to drink a lot in the long hot summers. And, as Bella started to climb, the hot, nor-west wind – that great dragon – came leaping to toss and tangle her. 'Go back! Go back! This is my kingdom. I'm going to bake it brown,' cried the wind.

But Bella was brave. 'Get back you dragon!' she shouted, and kept on climbing.

The wind-dragon wasn't her only enemy. Halfway up the hill she had to fight her way through an army of wild gorse bushes, all waving flags of gold and pointing daggers at her. Now that the trees were gone gorse had taken over. But Bella, twisting right, swinging left, slid safely between the daggers and ran on up the hill.

At the very top of the hill was the last tree, blackened on one side, but with one green branch still growing out of its burned trunk. When that branch saw Bella coming, it tossed its mane and reared up, defying the nor-west dragon.

Bella stroked its mane. Then, from the black cleft in the bottom of the trunk she took out stirrups of rope and her sacking saddle, saddled the branch, and swung herself astride it. Twigs, green with summer leaves, growing up along the last arch of living wood, seemed to bend back towards her. As Bella began her springing and bouncing they brushed against her face.

'Come on Greenmane! Gallop! Gallop!' cried Bella.

Greenmane leaped and curveted. Bella sang her song. The nor-west dragon tried to snatch the words before she could sing them, but she knew them too well. Off she went, galloping across whole countries and leaping mountain ranges. Her song vanquished the gorse army: its daggers shrank back from her. If she hadn't been there, singing her song of triumph, gorse would probably have covered Izanda by now. The whole hill would be nothing but dust for the nor-west dragon to fling up into the air. Bella held her arms high and shouted with triumph.

And then it happened! It had happened yesterday and it happened again now. Bella's feet touched the ground. She was growing just a little tall for Greenmane's grandest galloping.

'Hello,' said a voice behind her. 'Great day for a ride!'

A strange woman was watching her.

Bella immediately felt shy. She did not want anyone else to see her riding or hear her songs. But the woman stood on a rock staring around at the hills and out to sea until Bella felt restful in her silent company.

'It used to be a volcano you know,' the woman said at last, waving at the hills. 'Now it's a harbour.'

'It used to be a forest,' Bella told the woman, 'and now it's grass and gorse. I was singing enemies away.'

The woman looked properly at Bella for

the first time.

'I'll need your singing,' she said, smiling. 'This is going to be a farm from now on.'

'What will your animals drink?' cried Bella.

The woman laughed, and held out her hand. Bella took it and shook it. 'Name's Peg!' the woman said. 'Peg Halliday. My great-great-grandfather once burnt the bush on this hill. Now I've bought the hill back again. I'm going to have a tree farm.'

'What trees?' asked Bella.

'All sorts. I'm going to cover the whole hill in woodlots. Pine trees, of course. Everyone grows pines. Australian gum trees! English oaks – though they do grow so slowly. Walnuts! And a lot of the New Zealand trees that were growing here before the tree-burners came.'

'The gorse will try and swallow them all,'

said Bella. 'The gorse and the nor-wester want to conquer Izanda.'

'We'll fight back,' said Peg. 'We tree-warriors will protect Izanda.' She patted Greenmane. 'Keep riding! And keep on with that singing!' No one had ever asked Bella to keep on singing. Usually they told her to stop that noise.

Over the next months Bella often saw Peg moving around in the distance, planting trees, perhaps, or (dressed in overalls and a mask) spraying the gorse, driving it back towards the sea. Sometimes Peg worked alone. Sometimes she had other people helping her . . . students or travellers who wanted a job for three or four days. She planted a slope of pine trees and then a small patch of oaks. She planted windbreaks of quick-growing acacias. She planted the native New Zealand trees with the singing names . . . manuka and kanuka, totara and pohutukawa.

Every now and then Peg would climb up to look at the view and talk to Bella. They even planted a few trees together, singing as they planted.

'Old gorse won't bother little trees,' said Peg. 'It gets all leggy and lets the light in. It even protects them from the wind while they're small. But then the trees grow through the gorse which shrinks back from them. It'll take years, but in the end there'll be nowhere for the gorse to go.'

The nor-west dragon breathed on them. Its breath was like fire.

'It will take more than a few trees to tame me,' it whispered in Bella's ear.

And one afternoon that wind became more than a dragon. It became a true demon.

At the bottom of the hillside it had seemed to be an ordinary nor-wester strong (well, *very* strong) yet still ordinary. But as Bella came out on the top of the hill it suddenly struck her with a hot fist, bowling her backwards into the long grass. Bella staggered to her feet once more. 'I'll show you!' she shouted to the wind. 'You won't beat me.'

'I'll blow those little trees out of the earth. I'll scorch their roots off them,' screamed the wind. 'You'll see!'

But Bella leaped on to Greenmane, and off she went, leaping . . . leaping . . . The dragon bared its red-hot teeth at her but Bella began to sing a song of victory. She sang of the ancient forests of Izanda. She sang the song of a tree heroine protecting her people. The dragon leaped at her again and again but Bella locked her legs around Greenmane and clung on. She and the dragon wrestled furiously. As Greenmane and Bella sprang up the dragon dived under them. As Bella and Greenmane dived down the dragon sprang over them. 'One more leap, oh noble horse!' cried Bella, and they leaped again – leaped right through the hot heart of the wind-dragon.

The wind-dragon shrank back from them. The air grew still.

And then there was splintering . . . a cracking. Greenmane tumbled away beneath Bella. He disappeared. When she picked herself up out of the tangled grass there was nothing but a broken branch lying under her – the last, dying bough of a dead tree.

'Are you all right?' called a voice. Bella picked herself up slowly. Blood was running down her shaking legs. 'Come down to my shed,' said Peg. 'I've got sticking plaster there.'

Bella followed Peg down, down, down to the shed on the edge of the sea. There was a newly fenced paddock beside the shed and a new tank ready to catch any rain-water that might run from the shed roof.

They washed the scratches clean, blotting them until they stopped bleeding.

'I thought that wind would tear all my little trees out of the ground,' said Peg. 'But it's dropped right away. You must have sung wonderfully well.'

'Greenmane's gone. Gone forever,' said Bella. Her voice came out trembly. 'I didn't realise I was as heavy as all that.'

'I think he might have been making way for the next thing,' said Peg. 'Look! I've had that strip out there fenced in. It's because I'm getting a horse myself . . . two horses actually, because horses like company. And I'm not a rider – not yet. I like the idea of riding, but I'll have to take lessons and I'll need someone to help me keep those horses exercised. I wonder if your mum would let you take riding lessons with me. Then we could go over the island tracks, walking and riding.'

'And singing,' said Bella eagerly. 'We have to sing. And I can help you plant a few trees. I've had a bit of practice already.'

'And if we ride and sing well,' said Peg, 'one of these days we'll ride over the island

and we'll be riding through the new forest of
Izanda.'

'Riding and singing!' said Bella. 'Sharon
and Hamish might see me.'

'Is that a problem?' asked Peg.

'No way!' Bella cried. She almost sang it in
her best Izanda voice. 'They'll never be able to
say I can't sing or ride again.'

The Fox
by
Ted Hughes

The Fox is a jolly farmer and we
   farm the same land
He's a hardworking farmer, with a
   farmer's hard hand.

In the corn he farms hares – and
   what wallopers he rears!
And he plans his poultry system
   while a-feeling their ears.

In the pond he farms ducks, and a
few Christmas geese.
He's an eye for their meat, for their
down, for their grease.

In the hayfield it's marvellous the
flocks of his voles
And everywhere in the hedges fat
rats in their holes.

And everywhere in the hedges,
partridges lay clutches
Of eggs for his collection, and
some he lets hatch. He's

71

Ted Hughes

A hardworking farmer and we farm
   the same ground.
In our copse he tills rabbits worth
   many a pound,

And sometimes a cash-crop of
   squawking young crows.
In the old wood it's beetles he lifts
   with his nose.

And out on the pasture he borrows
   my rams,
And my pedigree ewes, for his
   pedigree lambs.

It's a Dog's Life
by
Michael Morpurgo

Open one eye. Same old basket, same old kitchen. Another day. That cocky little cockerel is at it again, crowing himself silly outside. Hasn't he got anything better to do?

Ear's itching. Good scratch. Lovely. Have a stretch. Have a good yawn. I need to go out. I've got things to do. Bark a bit, whine a bit, yelp a bit. Baby's crying. That's good. That'll get her up. Here comes herself down the stairs in her fluffy slippers, in her flappy dressing gown. 'Out you go Russ, you ragged rascal you. Go chase yourself.' No need to be like that. She's always so grumpy first thing in the mornings. Out I go.

Quick drink in my favourite puddle. Smarty's barking his 'good morning' at me from across the valley. Good old Smarty. Best friend I've got, except Lula – but then she's not a dog. I bark mine back, so there's two 'good mornings' echoing over the fields. Likes a good cat-chase does Smarty, just like me, though I prefer rabbits.

Can't hang about. There's work to do. Under the gate and off out into the field. There's the cows, busy grazing, but they're shifting already. They can feel me coming, even before they look. I'm at them, hustling them on, snapping at their heels. Good run. Good fun. Himself likes them ready by the yard gate by the time he comes down milking. He'll shout at me if they're not there. They're moving on nicely now.

It's a Dog's Life

There's a couple mooing at me and tossing
their heads. Pay no attention. All talk. That
one with the new calf. She's a bit skippy.
Watch her. She'll get nasty if I'm not careful.
Lie down a bit, nose in the grass. Give her the
hard eye. Give her time to think about it. She's
thought about it. There she goes, in amongst
the rest now. And here comes himself singing
his way down to the dairy, opening the gate for
the cows as he goes. 'Good dog,' he says and I
give him a wag of my tail. He likes that. So he
gives me another 'good dog' and a pat, and my
milk from the tank. Lovely.

Off back up to the house. Don't want to
miss breakfast, do I? Lula's already scoffing
her bacon and egg. I give her my very best
begging look. It always works. Two bacon
rinds in secret under the table, and all her toast
crusts too. There's good pickings under the

baby's chair this morning. I hoover it all up.

Lula always likes me to go with her to the end of the lane. She loves a cuddle before the school bus comes. She buries her head in my neck. It's the big squeeze today. 'Oh Russ,' she whispers. 'A horse. It's all I want for my birthday. I don't want a cake with silly candles on. I just want a horse.' And I'm thinking – What's so great about a horse? Isn't a dog good enough? Along comes the bus and on she gets. 'See you,' she says. And she's gone.

Someone's whistling for me. Himself again. Then he's shouting, 'Where are you, you ragged rascal you?' I'm coming. I'm coming. Back up the lane, through the hedge, over the gate. There he is. Sit at his feet. Look at him adoringly. He likes that. 'Well don't just sit there with your tongue hanging out.' There's some folk you just can't please. 'I

want those sheep in for shearing. Get at it.'
And all the while he keeps whistling and
whooping at me. I don't know why he
bothers. I know what I'm doing. Does he
think I haven't done this before? Doesn't he
know this is what I'm made for?

I hare down the hill, leap the stream and
get right around behind them. Keep low, keep
tight to the hedges. Don't spook them, but
don't let up on them. Be everywhere at once.
Bunch them. Huddle them. Nip at the

wanderers – not to hurt them, just to remind
them who's boss. No barking. Down. On your
belly. Don't rush them over the stream. That's
good. That's fine. Just that same old speckly
faced ewe making trouble. She's turning,
stamping her foot at me. Stare her out. She'll
go. Lose her and you could lose the lot. Easy
now. Easy. She's going. They're all going.
She's the last of them across the stream. Up
the hill they go towards himself over the top.
He's still at his whistling. The whole flock of

them are trotting along nicely now. Just perfect. And I'm slinking along behind, my eye on every one of them, my bark and my bite deep inside their heads. 'Good dog,' I get. Third one today. Not bad.

They look so silly without their wool. I watch the shearing from the top of the hay barn. Smells of mouse and rat. Lovely. I can hear them rustling. But I'm too tired to hunt them. Good place to sleep this, soft, warm. Tigger's been here too. She's somewhere hereabouts. I know she is. There she is up on the rafter, cool as you like, washing her whiskers. She's teasing me. I'll show her, I'll show her. Later, I'll do it later. Sleep now. Snuggle. Nose under tail. Lovely.

'Russ! Where are you Russ? Where's that ragged rascal of a dog? I know you're up there. I want these sheep out. Move yourself.' Down

I go, and out they go, in a great muddle bleating at each other, picking fights, bopping one another. They don't recognise each other without their clothes on. Not very bright, that's the trouble with sheep.

Lunch in the kitchen. I have what they have, but I eat it ten times faster. No doubt about it, I'm a champion chomper. No water in my bowl – they're always forgetting. So back to my puddle. But there's a pig in it. Rolling. Best not to disturb her. There's plenty of other puddles.

Will you look at that! There's hundreds of crows out in the mown hay field. Well, I'm not having that. Who do they think they are? Chase them all off, send them all cawing skywards, back where they belong. Cackle away. See if I care.

What's this? What's this? Fox smell! Fresh. He was here this morning. I follow the

trail of him down through the bluebell wood to his den. He's down there, deep down. I can smell him. But smelling him isn't half as much fun as chasing him. This place is the best on the farm for smells – badger, deer, rabbit – all sorts. I make my way through the wood, following the scent of deer down to the river. I stand there in the water and lap. Better than puddle water anytime. I have a bit of a swim, climb out and shake myself dry in the sun. Have a good wash. Stretch out in the sun. A fish plops in the river. And another one. Out of the corner of my eye, I see a heron move. Leave him be. Sleep.

Smarty wakes me, snuffling in my ear. He knows right away what I'm thinking. I know what he's thinking. Tigger. We'll go on a Tigger hunt. We find her soon enough, skulking in the garden. Over the wall we send her. She skitters across the farmyard, round the back of the tractor, past the dung heap, out into the field. We're catching her up all the time. Closer. Closer. We've got her this time. Oh cats! The tree. Somehow she always finds a tree. Up she goes. I can't climb trees, nor can Smarty. But we can both bark our heads off. And Tigger lies along the branch above us, hissing at us like a snake. Good fun. Bit puffed out though.

Tractor's coming. Smarty's gone already. He knows they don't like him about the place. 'Russ, where were you, Russ? Been looking all over for you. Pigs have got out again. I had to fetch them back without you. What's the point in keeping a dog and barking myself, eh? You ragged old rascal you.' That's three ragged rascals today, and three good dogs. Why can't he make up his mind? 'Hop up. At least you can help me put the calves out.'

Nothing worse than moving young calves. Maybe they think I'm going to eat them. They just don't seem to understand what I'm there for. All excited they are, tails high, all tippy-toed and skippy. Pretty things though. Pity they get so big and lumpy when they get older.

Back to the end of the lane to meet Lula. I'm a bit late. She's there already swinging her bag and singing. 'Happy birthday to me, happy birthday to me. Happy birthday, dear Lula, happy birthday to me!'

For tea there's a big cake with candles on it, and they're singing that song again. Will you look at them tucking into that cake! And never a thought for me. Lula's so busy unwrapping her presents that she doesn't even notice I'm there, not even when I rest my head on her knee.

Car! Car coming up our lane, and not one

I know. I'm out of the house in a flash and biting at the tyres. There's a trailer behind. Have a go at that too. I'm not just a farm dog, I'm a guard dog, and whoever it is had better know I mean business.

'Russ! Russ! Stop it, you ragged rascal you.' That's all the thanks I get for doing my job. I'm telling you, it's a dog's life. Lula's holding her hands over her eyes as they let the back of the trailer down. Looks like a horse. He's coming down the ramp, backwards. He's jet black with a white ribbon tied around his neck. Give him a sniff. Horse. Definitely horse. Lula takes her hands away. She goes mad. She's hugging everyone in sight, except me. She goes up to the horse, puts her arms round his neck and hugs him, just like she hugs me, only for longer. 'Beautiful. Beautiful,' she says. 'Just what I always wanted.'

Well, I'm not staying where I'm not wanted. I'm off. There's that cake on the table in the kitchen, and there's lots of it left. It smells delicious, and I haven't had any. Up on the chair. Help yourself. Lick the plate clean. But the plate falls off the table and smashes, noisily, and they all come running. I look dead innocent. 'You thieving little rascal, you. No supper for you tonight.' They kick me out. I don't care. It was worth it. It was *so* good. I go and sit at the top of the hill and tell Smarty all about it. He barks back. 'Good on you. Who wants to be a good dog anyway?'

Then Lula's sitting down beside me and putting her arm around me. 'I really love my horse,' she says, 'but I love you more. Promise.' Give her a good lick. Make her giggle. I like it when she giggles. She tastes of cake. Lick her again. Lovely.

Brook Dancer
by
Gillian Cross

Robert had two grandmothers.

Grandma Helen was tiny and smart and good at making things. She built cupboards and designed her own clothes and cooked the best cakes in Newcastle.

Granny Jo was big and untidy. Her cakes sank, her curtains were crooked and she hardly knew which end to hold a hammer.

But she had a brook outside her house, running through the middle of the village. When Robert stayed there, he paddled, and fed the ducks, and fished for tiddlers. Sometimes he and Granny Jo walked to the far end of the village, where the brook flowed into the River Avon. They stood on the bank and looked for kingfishers.

Grandma Helen knew all about the brook, because Robert told her. One day, she sent a huge parcel with a letter, just before Robert went off to stay with Granny Jo in Somerset.

> *Dear Robert,*
> *I made this for you to sail on Granny Jo's brook.*
> *Love from Grandma Helen*

Inside the parcel was a beautiful wooden sailing ship with two masts and real sails. The rudder moved, and the lifebelts had the ship's name painted on them. *Brook Dancer*.

The keel stuck down and the masts stuck

up. Altogether, the ship was almost as tall as Robert.

'Oh dear!' said his mother. 'You can tell Grandma Helen's never seen that brook.'

'Why?' Robert said.

His father laughed. 'How far up your boots does the water come when you paddle there?'

Robert thought. 'Just over the toes.'

His mother nodded. 'That's not nearly enough to float this ship. There's no point in taking it to Granny Jo's.'

'But I've got to! Grandma Helen *said*!'

Robert wouldn't let them leave it behind. It was too big for his suitcase, so he carried it out to the car in his arms. All the way to Granny Jo's, he held it on his lap. It was a miserable journey and it rained all the way.

When Granny Jo saw the ship, she shook her head. 'It's lovely, but it won't sail on the brook. We could try it on the river, when the weather's better.'

'Not the river,' Robert said.

The river was too deep for paddling. If he couldn't paddle along beside the ship, it might float out of reach. Then it would sail all the way down to the sea and be lost for ever.

'It's for the *brook*,' he said stubbornly. 'Look at the *name*.'

Granny Jo smiled. 'Let's see what happens when the sun comes out.'

She and Robert waved goodbye to Robert's parents. Then they had scrambled egg and cocoa before bedtime. All the time, the rain swished against the cottage windows.

'Quite a storm,' Granny Jo said. 'I hope it doesn't keep you awake.'

'It won't,' Robert said. He was so tired that his eyes were closing as he walked upstairs. He was almost asleep before Granny Jo turned out the light.

She peeped through the curtains. 'The brook's very full. There *might* be enough water to sail your ship tomorrow. But I hope it stops raining soon, so the water goes down.'

Then she said goodnight, and Robert fell asleep.

But sometime after midnight, the storm stopped. No more rain beating on the glass. No more wind roaring over the roof of the cottage. The silence woke Robert up and he opened his eyes and thought, I wonder if there's enough water in the brook. He slid out of bed and padded across to the window.

The brook was full. The water was swirling right up to the top of the banks. Fantastic! he thought.

Then he remembered what Granny Jo had

said. *I hope it stops raining soon, so the water goes down.* It had stopped raining already. Would all the water be gone by the morning?

He couldn't bear that! But he knew Granny Jo wouldn't let him go outside in the middle of the night to sail his ship.

Almost without deciding, he found himself creeping down the stairs. He pulled on his coat and boots, unlocked the door and picked up *Brook Dancer*.

Outside, it was very dark. He tiptoed across the footpath, on to the grass beside the brook. The water had overflowed there, but he paddled through it and leaned forward to put his ship into the water.

He hadn't realised how slippery the wet grass was. His foot skidded and he grabbed at the bank. He saved himself from falling into the water, but he couldn't help squealing.

And when he scrambled up, *Brook Dancer* had gone. The water was sweeping her away towards the end of the village street. Beyond that, the brook flowed across a field, right into the River Avon.

And on to the sea.

Robert started to run, slopping along in his boots. Almost at once, he slipped over again. This time, the water on the grass was deeper. His boots filled up and his clothes got wet. He started to shiver, but he pulled himself up and squelched on.

He didn't get far. A door banged, and Granny Jo came racing up behind him.

'Robert! What are you *doing*?'

'I'm trying to get my –'

She didn't listen. She scooped him up and actually *carried* him back to the cottage, scolding all the way.

'Look at you! You're freezing. It's lucky I heard you shriek. You could have drowned! No, don't argue! You're going straight into a warm bath!'

She didn't let Robert speak, until he'd had the bath and he was sitting by the fire, dressed in lots of warm clothes.

'*Now* you can talk,' she said. 'What were you up to?'

'M-my ship,' Robert's voice shook, even though he wasn't cold any more. 'I went out to sail it –'

'In the middle of the *night?*' Granny Jo said.

'I thought the water might be gone by the morning. But –' Robert bit his lip and stopped.

Granny Jo patted his hand. 'Never mind. You're safe now. But you've left your ship outside. I'd better fetch it in.'

She stood up and went to the front door. But when she opened it, she gasped. The brook had overflowed completely. The water was almost at her front doorstep.

Robert gasped too. 'You said the water would go *down* if it stopped raining.'

'Not until it's all run off the hills,' said Granny Jo.

'But if it gets any higher – it'll come into the house.'

'We must get the sandbags out of the shed. And put the furniture up on bricks.' Granny Jo was pulling on her boots. 'But I must warn everyone else first.'

She picked up her torch and went outside. Robert heard her splashing along the row of cottages, knocking and shouting, 'Wake up! The brook's flooding!'

By the time she came back, Robert had

already dragged the sandbags out of the shed.

'What a good boy you are,' she said. 'I'll take them round to the front when I've got your ship. Where did you leave it?'

Robert looked down at his feet. 'It sailed away,' he said, in a small voice. 'Down the brook.' And then, in an even smaller voice, 'Towards the river.'

'Oh dear,' Granny Jo said. 'Oh *dear*.' She looked at him. 'Do you mind very much?'

Robert stared hard at the floor. 'Does the river really go all the way to the sea?' he mumbled.

Granny Jo didn't answer straight away. She looked round her cottage, at the carpet and the piano and the big, soft armchairs. Then she looked back at Robert.

'Put my mac on,' she said. 'We'll go and

look for *Brook Dancer*. Perhaps she's caught in the reeds somewhere.'

'But what about your furniture?' Robert said.

'Maybe the sandbags will keep out the water until we get back.'

They carried them round and piled them up outside the front door. Then they splashed off along the street, keeping close to the cottages, where the water was shallow. As they went, Granny Jo shone her torch across at the brook. But there was no sign of *Brook Dancer*.

'The water's still rising,' Granny Jo said, in a worried voice. 'I can't think why it's so high. It didn't rain *that* much.'

At the end of the street, she stopped. Robert looked across the field, feeling cold and miserable. The water looked deeper out there. Were they going to turn back?

Granny Jo smiled. 'I'll have to give you

a piggyback,' she said. 'Take the torch and
hop up.'

She walked very slowly across the field, taking care not to slip. The water would have been over the top of Robert's boots, but it only came halfway up hers.

'Keep looking,' she said.

Robert shone the torch towards the brook. There were lots of things floating on it. Cans and carrier bags and even a plastic duck. But there was no sign of *Brook Dancer*.

'I'm sorry, darling,' said Granny Jo. 'I'm afraid you've lost it. And I don't think I can carry you much further.'

'Could we just go to the river?' Robert said.

Granny Jo sighed. 'The water's getting deeper all the time. We've got to turn back. Can't you see the river from here?'

Robert shone the torch straight ahead. He could see the clumps of reeds on the river bank. The ship *had* to be in one of them.

But it wasn't.

Granny Jo began to turn. The torch beam swung along the river, towards the place where the brook joined it . . .

And suddenly Robert saw a sail!

'Granny! Stop!'

Brook Dancer was stuck there, with lots of other things. Cans and bottles and sticks. They couldn't get out into the river, because there was a big bush blocking the way, with its roots sticking up in the air.

'It's like a dam!' Granny Jo said. 'No wonder the brook's flooding.'

'What can we do?' said Robert.

'Shout,' said Granny Jo. 'Or all the cottages will flood. Shine the torch across the brook, at Mr Critchley's farmhouse.'

Robert shone it, and she bellowed, 'Sam

Critchley! Over here!! Help!!!'

Nothing happened.

Robert shouted too. 'MR CRITCHLEY! HELP!!!'

Another torch gleamed suddenly, across the brook. A voice bellowed back. 'What's up?'

'The brook's blocked!' yelled Granny Jo.

'OK,' Mr Critchley shouted. 'Hang on!'

Granny Jo carried Robert up to the edge of the field, where the water was shallower. 'Hold on to the fence,' she said. 'Don't let go for anything.'

She waded back to meet Mr Critchley and his three sons. They were carrying rakes to pull the blockage out of the brook.

'Mind the ship!' Granny Jo shouted. 'Let me get that first!'

She waded deeper, to pull it out. When she came back to Robert, she was shaking her head. '*Brook Dancer*'s saved us all from flooding,' she said. 'But I'm afraid her sails are torn and both her masts have snapped.'

Robert didn't care. He took his lovely ship and held it tight. 'Grandma Helen can mend those,' he said.

Grandma Helen did. She made new sails and new masts and she fixed a long cord to the back of the ship, for Robert to hold when *Brook Dancer* sailed on the river.

But it was Granny Jo who made the best thing of all. A flag for the main mast, embroidered with wobbly, uneven letters. Robert loved it, even though she hadn't got it quite right. It said

HERO OF THE FLOD

Swallows
by
Ted Hughes

I'll say this for swallows, they're
    marvellous workers.
You think they're sunning by the
    pond – but no!
They're down there gathering balls of
    mud – in their mouths!
They're building their huts with their
    beaks!

You see them looping all the
    directions of the compass
Into a floral bow, and all day
It looks like skater's truant play. It is not.
It's full-tilt, all-out labour, stoking
    their nestful.

Ted Hughes

You'd think they'd play a bit, after,
    with their family –
All figure-flying together. No – they
    stick at it.
Brood after brood – right up to
    Michaelmas
The crib's a quiverful of hungry arrows.

They must go round the whole globe
    twenty times
Just among my buildings. Marvellous!
The truest, keenest, bluest blade-metal,
Whetted on air, every move smoother –

The finest tool on the farm!

The Hen and Bull Story
by
Jan Mark

'Where are we going?' Joseph said, in his special back-seat whine. He was sitting next to Anna. Mum was in front with Granny, who was driving.

They had been in the car for almost an hour. Every five minutes Joseph said, '*Where* are we going?'

'We're going to see where Mum lived when she was little – as little as you,' Anna said, because Joseph took more notice if you talked about him.

'I want a drink,' Joseph said. He hadn't listened to what she was saying and in five minutes he would start again. '*Where* are we going?'

'You can have a drink when we stop,' Mum said, over her shoulder. 'We're nearly there.'

'Where are we nearly?'

'Where I lived when I was little.'

That meant nothing to Joseph. Mum had never been little. Mum was Mum, Granny was Granny, Anna was Anna. He knew that *he* was getting bigger, but everyone else stayed the same for ever and ever.

The place they were going to see was the village where Granny and Grandpa had lived when Mum was Joseph's age and Granny was the same age as Mum was now. Even Anna could hardly get her head around that idea, although she had seen photographs. Granny young? Never.

'Oh! There's the holly tree.' Mum was

looking out of the window, pointing. 'There's the post-box – and the pond. That's funny. I thought the pond was further on.'

'There is no further on,' Granny said, and stopped the car outside a garden gate with a name on it: *Lane End*. 'This is it.'

'But it can't be, it used to take ages to walk to the post.'

'It took *you* ages,' Granny said. 'I could be there and back in five minutes.'

Granny and Mum got out and unbuckled Anna and Joseph. Joseph needed help but Anna scrambled out and stood by Mum, looking at the garden gate, *Lane End*, and the cottage beyond it at the end of the lane.

'It's so small,' Mum was saying. 'I thought it was a house.'

'No such luck,' Granny said, standing Joseph on his feet. 'Two rooms up, two down, and the bathroom built on at the back. Remember the bathroom?'

'I remember the beetles.'

'Where were the beetles?' Anna asked.

'In the bath, mainly,' Granny said, grimly.

Mum took the picnic bag out of the boot. 'Look, there are still teazels growing in the big field,' she said. 'Only it's not so big.'

'Drink,' Joseph pleaded, in a suffering voice.

'Any second now, grizzly-bear,' Granny said, and picked him up. They climbed over the stile at the end of the lane, into the big field that was not so big after all. It looked big enough to Anna. There was a path among the teazels and thistles and they followed it in single file, Granny carrying Joseph on her shoulders, clear of the scratchy bits. The thistles were taller than Anna. The teazels were taller than Mum. Everything was taller than Joseph.

On the far side of the field was a little clump of trees and a patch of long grass. From the grassy place they could see out across fields, but there was nothing to look at — except the fields.

'There aren't many trees left,' Mum said. 'This used to be a whole wood.'

Granny sat Joseph down and gave him his orange juice. 'No,' she said. 'It was always like this. And don't tell me the trees have shrunk.'

Mum unpacked the bag. They were not having a proper picnic, just a drink and fruit and biscuits because Joseph hated going anywhere unless there was food at the end of it. Anna just wanted a drink after the long dry journey. Mum and Granny hardly bothered to drink. They kept looking around and pointing

at things and saying, 'Do you remember . . .'

'The trees haven't shrunk,' Mum said. 'They must have grown. You can't see Earley's Farm any more.'

Granny stood up. 'Of course you can –' she started to say, but then she stopped and stared. She walked a little way down the path, and back again. She looked surprised and sad.

'You're right, it isn't there,' she said. 'They must have knocked it down.'

'They can't have. There's the barn,' Mum said. 'I remember the barn.'

'Well, the house has gone,' Granny said. 'This must all be part of another farm now. That barn's still being used. There's a tractor in it.'

'Did you used to go to the farm?' Anna asked Mum. 'Did you play with the lambs and stroke the horses and give them sugar?' She had only seen farms in picture books.

'They didn't have horses,' Mum said. 'Did they? I don't remember horses. Why did we go there?'

'To buy eggs. Mrs Earley kept hens. She had a stall by the gate. Do you remember the Earleys?'

'I remember the stall. It used to have jars of pickled onions on it. And I remember the hens.'

'Do you remember the bull?'

'Did they have a bull?'

'Did they have a bull?' Granny said. 'You *don't* remember, do you? We went over there one day to collect the eggs and when I looked round you'd wandered off. "Oh, I shouldn't worry," Mrs Earley said. "She can't come to any mischief, she's only been gone a moment."'

'How old were you?' Anna said. This sounded as if it was going to be a story about Mum getting into trouble.

'She was nearly three,' Granny said. 'Just a bit younger than Joseph. Well, I wasn't sure she hadn't got into mischief. I knew how fast she could move. And just then Mr Earley, the farmer, came round the corner, looking very pale. "Here," he said to me. "Do you know where your daughter is? She's down the end of the field, feeding greengages to the bull."'

'What's a greengage?' Anna said.

'A sort of plum. You'd think it was sour, being green, but they're very sweet when they're ripe. Mrs Earley went as green as a gage herself. "Not *in* the field, is she?"

'"You come and look," said Mr Earley, and we went to the gate, and there was your mum, in the middle of the field, right up next to the bull, feeding him with greengages out of a paper bag. She'd got it off the stall by the gate.'

'Greengages? You're making this up,' Mum said.

'Oh, no I'm not,' Granny said. 'I've never been so scared. We all stood in a row by the gate, afraid to move in case we startled the bull and he attacked you, or just knocked you down and trampled on you. You were so small and he was so big he'd never have noticed.'

'What was his name?' Joseph said.

'Who? What was who's name?'

'The bull.'

'I wasn't very bothered about his name just then,' Granny said. 'I don't know what I was thinking of, but I climbed over the gate and started to walk towards you and you went on standing there and the bull went on eating his greengages. When I got to you I said, very quietly, "I've got the eggs, it's time to go home," and I was praying you wouldn't do what you usually did.'

'What did you usually do?' Anna asked Mum.

'She used to sit down and scream,' Granny said, when Mum didn't answer. 'And I could see she was just about to, so I said, "Mr Earley's got some more greengages, let's go and get them," and I took her hand and walked back to the gate, very slowly, and I could hear the bull walking after us, very slowly, breathing hard through his nose, all the way. Then I lifted her over the gate to Mrs Earley and climbed over as well and the bull snorted and stamped. I suppose he wanted more greengages. And then he cantered away with his tail up.'

'Was he dangerous?' Anna said. She had seen pictures of angry bulls pawing the ground, blowing steam from their nostrils.

'He must have weighed half a tonne,' Granny said. 'If he'd just rolled over and waved his legs in the air he could have squashed us flat. Don't you remember it at all?'

'Well, now you mention it, I do remember the bull,' Mum said. 'Wasn't he red and white?'

'That's right. A Hereford. After that, I never let go of your hand when we went to get the eggs.'

'Oh, yes you did,' Mum said. 'Once you did. I remember *that*.'

'When?'

'My third birthday. We went for the eggs and I had new shoes on. Mrs Earley was feeding the chickens in the hen yard and I wanted her to see my shoes, so I went right in to show her. Only she didn't notice me so she came out and shut the gate and there I was locked in with all those enormous savage hens. And the cockerel. He was as tall as I was.'

'Hens aren't enormous and savage,' Anna said.

'They are if you're only three,' Mum said. 'They were all rushing for their food and I was in the way. And the cockerel came over to see what was going on in case someone was upsetting his girls, and I screamed and panicked and all the hens screamed and panicked and the cockerel stood on his toes and flapped his wings – that was when you and Mrs Earley saw what was going on. I was trying to climb up the gate by then. I was sure

I could feel hot hen's breath on my legs.'

'I don't remember that at all,' Granny said. 'What happened?'

'Mrs Earley opened the gate and let me out and the hens all went back to having breakfast,' Mum said. 'I never let go of your hand, after that. Do you really not remember?'

'Well, you don't remember the bull.'

'I wasn't frightened of the bull,' Mum said. 'And you weren't frightened of the chickens.'

'Yes,' Granny said, 'but the bull was dangerous. You could have been killed. I don't think the hens would have hurt you.'

'I didn't know that,' Mum said. 'Any more than I knew that the bull might have flattened me. That's why I remember the hens and not the bull, and you remember the bull and not the hens.'

'Have we all finished eating?' Granny said. 'Let's go and look at the church. I don't think that will have changed.'

They packed the bag again and walked back along the prickly path between the teazels. Joseph was telling himself a story.

'One-pon-time, there was a big bad hen. And it sat down on a poor little bull and squashed it flat.'

'See what I mean?' said Mum.

Anna and Joseph sang, 'Who's afraid of the big bad hen?' all the way back to the car.

Mona
by
Jamila Gavin

'**M**eet Mona!'

Uncle Cedric stood in the doorway holding a leash. The light from the hallway fell on him, but it trailed away into darkness behind him, so they couldn't quite see what was on the end of the leash.

'Oh great! It's a dog!' cried Duane, who had always wanted a dog.

'Bags I walk him,' shouted Saffron, as usual trying to be the first to stake a claim.

'Her,' corrected Uncle Cedric.

The children rushed outside excitedly.

But when they saw what was on the end of the lead, they stopped short. Duane backed away uncertainly till he reached his mother's side. Saffron just stood there staring, dumbstruck for once. Molotov, their cat, looked electrified and fled.

'Well, you'd better come in,' said Mum. She was still feeling half cross because she had let Uncle Cedric twist her arm and agreed to look after his pet for a week while he went away. She realised he hadn't told her what kind of pet, but Uncle Cedric had always had dogs, so she assumed it was a dog.

Being a very house-proud sort of a mum, she didn't care for dogs. They left hair everywhere and a strong smell – especially after a walk in the rain. She was a cat person. But Uncle Cedric had always been so generous with them in the past, she felt she couldn't refuse.

'I can't stop,' said Uncle Cedric. 'My car's on a yellow line, and in any case, I'm a bit on the late side. Look, here's everything you need.' He thrust a large holdall into the hallway. 'It's got her feeding bowl, pet food, you know biscuits, cereal and things – but, really, she eats anything except meat. She's vegetarian. Otherwise, give her your leftovers. Whatever. Oh – and I've put in a whole bag of mini Mars Bars. She's very partial to those. You can make her do anything with a Mars Bar.'

'Uncle,' said Saffron strangely. 'What kind of dog is that?' She peered into the gloom.

Uncle Cedric tugged the lead. Something black moved within the darkness. It came blinking into the light. 'Her name's Mona,' said Uncle Cedric. 'You know – after Mona Lisa. She's beautiful isn't she?'

She had large, flappy ears with pinky grey insides; she had a funny thin straight tail which fluffed out at the end, and four little cloven feet – only little – because they supported a great round belly which hung beneath a huge, shining, black, silky body. She gazed up at them with small squidgy eyes and a snuffling snout.

'She's a PIG!' yelled Mum, backing away, with Duane clinging to her skirts. 'I'm not having a pig in this house. You said it was a dog.'

'I never said it was a dog,' protested Uncle Cedric. 'Anyway, she's as good as a dog – better. She's called a Vietnamese pot-bellied pig.'

'I don't care what she's called, she's a PIG!' insisted Mum.

'I didn't know there were black pigs, only

pink pigs,' said Duane.

'This one's from Vietnam. They have black pigs there – they are very intelligent – probably more intelligent than you.'

'I thought pigs only lived on farms,' mumbled Saffron.

'Makes no difference,' retorted Uncle Cedric. 'She's a household pet. She can live anywhere.'

'She's huge,' Mum's voice rose in hopeless protest.

'But she's still loveable. Now look, I'm late – I'll miss my flight. I really must get on. There's nothing for you to do but feed her and take her for walks. Just treat her as if she were a dog. She's house-trained and she doesn't leave hairs all over the place. It's only for a week.' Uncle Cedric thrust the lead into Mum's hands. He dashed back to the car and returned carrying a large dog basket with a blanket. 'She can sleep in this.' He strode past them carrying everything into the kitchen and dumped it in a corner near the fridge. He knelt down in front of his pet, put his arms round her thick body and pressed his nose to her snout. 'Goodbye, Mona my sweetheart,' he drooled. 'See you in a week.' Then he fled.

'CEDRIC!' bellowed Mum.

'Don't forget the Mars Bars!' His voice yelled above the car engine, as he pulled away with a cheery wave.

They stood in the kitchen staring at Mona. Mona stared back.

'Who's Mona Lisa?' asked Duane.

'She's a painting,' muttered Mum. 'A painting of a beautiful woman with a mysterious smile.'

'Oh.'

They looked again at Mona. 'I can't see a mysterious smile,' said Saffron.

The lead had trailed out of Mum's hands. Mona began to shuffle round the kitchen sniffing. Her snout was like a checkout machine, sliding over every object she could reach. When she got to the cupboard below the worktop, she eased her snout under the handle and just opened it.

'Oh no you don't!' cried Mum, leaping forward and grabbing the lead. 'Let's get her food out. She's probably hungry.'

They got out the bowls; one for the cereal and the other for water. They placed them side by side near the kitchen door. Mona *was* hungry. She stuck her snout into the bowl and swoosh, it was gone in one suck. She looked round for more and saw the cat's bowl. Molotov always knew when he'd had enough, and left what he didn't want. Mona stuck her snout in his bowl and swoosh! it was gone.

'Oh, she's one of those,' said Mum wearily. 'An eating machine. Well let's get her to bed.' She fixed her eye on Mona and pointed to the dog basket. 'Bed,' she commanded.

Mona rudely ignored her.

Mum grabbed her collar and tried to pull her over. 'Bed, Mona!' she repeated.

But though all three of them heaved against her, Mona didn't budge an inch.

'Uncle Cedric said she'd do anything for a Mars Bar,' said Duane digging his hand into the holdall for a Mars Bar. He ripped off the wrapper and held it over the basket. 'Here, Mona! Mars Bar!'

Mona turned like a guided missile and was in the basket in a flash.

'Good girl, Mona!' cheered Duane, daring to give her a pat.

Mona flopped an ear over an eye and looked coy.

'Where's Molotov?' Everyone looked around for the cat.

'He'll come when he's ready,' Mum reassured the children. 'He can take care of himself.'

'See you in the morning,' Mum gave Mona a reluctant smile. She switched out the kitchen light, firmly shut the door, and they all trooped up to bed.

The next morning. The next morning. The next . . .

It was like all hell had broken loose – yet silently – for no one heard a thing. Mum went down first as usual. She entered the kitchen and screamed; one great long terrible scream.

Saffron and Duane rushed down.

Everything had been tipped out of the fridge; everything had been tipped out of every single cupboard in the kitchen – even the upper cupboards. In the middle of the mayhem, with butter paper licked clean, and jam slurping out of jam-pots, and remains of eggshells, cartons, tins, vegetables and fruit, stood Mona, with her snout in a yogurt pot. She looked up at them and seemed to smile – a mysterious smile.

Mum found wings, flying around between Mona, who she managed to drag outside with the aid of a Mars Bar and tied to the apple tree, and rushing back to clear up the mess, make breakfast, yell at the kids to get ready for school and look for Molotov, who wouldn't be found.

They ate their breakfast standing up, then

Mum firmly shut all the cupboards and drawers. She propped a chair in front of the fridge and pushed the kitchen table as a barricade for the kitchen cupboards. Mona was brought in from the garden. 'Basket!' commanded Mum. Mona looked the other way.

'Mars Bar!' yelled the children throwing one into the basket, and Mona went in most obediently.

'Right, let's go!' cried Mum and slammed shut the door.

Mum was waiting for Saffron and Duane when school was over. They walked home. 'We'd better take Mona to the park,' said Mum. 'She's been in all day.'

Molotov was sitting on the doorstep when they arrived at the gate. He looked miffed, and didn't come down the path to greet them as usual. 'Poor Molotov. He doesn't like having Mona around.'

Inside, they stood before the kitchen door. 'It's funny to think there's a huge, black, Vietnamese pot-bellied pig on the other side of that door,' whispered Duane. Mum opened the door. 'Hello Mona, we're ho . . . AAAAAaaaaaH!'

Havoc. The chair in front of the fridge was tipped over and the fridge door was swinging open; all the cupboard doors were open top and bottom and, strewn across the floor, were the chewed, spewed, crunched, scrunched, ripped, stripped and gnawed remains of any tin, jar, carton or bag which had contained anything which could be eaten.

Where was Mona? They heard a deep snore. They didn't see her at first. She had gripped the end of the blanket in her teeth and

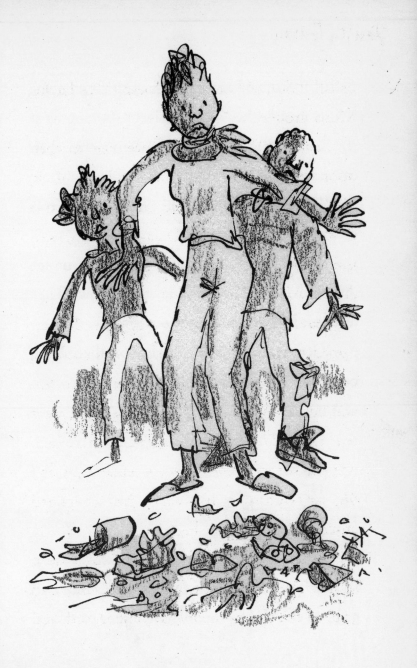

pulled it right up over her head. But there she was in her basket sound asleep, looking as if she had slept through the mayhem rather than caused it.

'How did she do it?' gasped Saffron looking around aghast.

Mona Lisa's head appeared from under the blanket. She opened an eye, showed her teeth and smiled a mysterious smile.

'Get her out of my sight, or there'll be bacon for breakfast,' yelled Mum.

So while Mum cleared up yet again, Saffron and Duane stuffed their pockets with Mars Bars and took Mona to the park. It took two of them to hold her. She was very strong. But she was as good as gold – so long as a Mars Bar was waved in front of her nose. She stopped at the zebra crossing, she didn't tug and try to chase the little Jack Russell who dashed up yapping and sniffing, and she didn't puncture the football which rolled up to her snout.

Quite a crowd gathered. Not many people take pigs for walks. 'My he's a grand fellow,' said one.

'She,' corrected Saffron.

'What's her name?' asked another.

'Mona. You know, after Mona Lisa,' announced Duane.

'Oh yeah! The lady with the smile.'

That night Mum said to Mona, 'It's the garden shed for you tonight, madam.'

'But Mum . . .' pleaded Saffron. 'She was ever so good in the park. Give her another chance. It'll be cold in the shed.'

Mum was adamant. Firmly, she led Mona up the garden to the wooden shed. Saffron and Duane followed in procession, carrying her basket and bowls. 'There's no food to be found here, madam,' she said icily. 'You'll just have to make do with what's in your bowl.'

Saffron and Duane moaned, 'Poor Mona.' But Molotov looked pleased, and slept in the kitchen that night.

Saffron had now decided she loved Mona, so she was the first to wake up the next morning. Her first thought was Mona. 'Fancy sleeping in that cold shed all night.' She ran downstairs and out into the garden. It was early. Only a few birds cheeped sleepily. The curtains were still drawn in all the surrounding houses. She got to the shed. The door was half open. The garden hose trailed out of it and disappeared across the lawn. Had Mum come out to water the garden early before work?

'Mona?' whispered Saffron, peering inside.

As the daylight flooded in, she saw the terrible sight. Mona had had a feast. She had chewed all the gumboots, ripped up the gardening gloves, mangled the straw hats, gnawed at the tool handles, spilled all the trays of seedlings, knocked over every jar, tin, bottle and, as for the garden hose . . . what had she done with the garden hose? Saffron followed it. It coiled round the apple tree, across the lawn, through a large hole in the fence (the day before it had just been a crack) into next door's garden, across a flattened flower bed, a tipped over bird table, all the way to the treasured vegetable patch of Mrs O'Connor. There lay Mona in a tangle, with the hose wrapped round her neck and legs, looking like a captured battleship. A half-chewed cabbage hung out of her mouth.

'Mona!' gulped Saffron. 'Oh Mona!'

Mona looked up at Saffron innocently and – well – just smiled a mysterious smile.

'This is war,' declared Mum.

She led Mona to the garage. She found a long chain and a padlock. She looped the chain through Mona's dog collar and attached it to a hook on the concrete wall, winding it round and round several times.

Mum took the children to school, and then went on to her job.

At the end of the day, when they all got back, Molotov came purring down the path to greet them. They went to the garage to see Mona.

Mona was sitting in her basket. The chain was still round her neck and still attached to the hook on the wall. No mayhem, no mess, everything was as they left it – except, 'I think she likes eating nuts and bolts,' murmured Duane who noticed a glittering store of them in her basket.

But Mum grinned with satisfaction. 'I

think I'm winning,' she said.

'Good girl, Mona!' shouted Saffron throwing her arms round the pig.

That night, after walking Mona in the park, Mum eased the car into the garage and left the pig chained again to the wall for the night. 'This is obviously the best place for her,' she said triumphantly.

'Goodnight Mona!' sighed Saffron, giving her a kiss. 'Be good.'

'Here's some Mars Bars for you,' soothed Saffron, dropping them in the basket.

It was the first morning it had been peaceful since Mona arrived. The kitchen was clean and immaculate when they all trooped down for breakfast; the garden was calm, and when Mum looked out and saw Molotov lazily prowling through the bushes, she knew all was right with the world. They had a leisurely breakfast, and then went to the garage to get the car and check on Mona.

The garage door was closed when Mum went over, but – not locked. Odd. Moments later she was rushing back in distress. The car was gone. So was Mona.

'What's up, Mum?' cried Saffron and Duane.

Mum was on the telephone. 'Police? My car! It's been stolen! And the pig . . .'

'A PIG?' repeated the police woman on the other end.

'Yes . . . no . . . I don't know! But she's gone too. The car is blue and six years old, registration J 296 F. The pig? She's a black – yes BLACK – a Vietnamese pot-bellied pig. She's called Mona, yes M-O-N-A, you know after Mona Lisa . . .'

*   *   *

The thief thought he was so clever. How silently he had broken into the garage. Easy peasy. People hardly ever locked their cars when they were in the garage. Cor! This one hadn't even shut the passenger door at the back. He closed it gently, and kicked in a chain which was hanging from the front. His torch flashed in the darkness as he opened the driver's door and released the handbrake. He would ease the car out into the road before starting it up.

Soon, he was off, speeding away through the empty neighbourhood heading for the country. He left the city streets behind with their harsh orange lights and roaming police cars. He hit the motorway and sighed with relief.

'A bit of energy, that's what I need,' he

murmured tearing off the wrapper of a Mars Bar . . . It was then he glanced in his rear mirror. A face loomed from the back. A black face, with great floppy ears, a nose more like a snout and two beady little eyes which gleamed like a demon. It smiled – a mysterious smile.

Later that day, the phone rang. It was the police. 'We've found your car, and your pig – and we caught the thief. At least the pig did. We found the thief blubbing his eyes out with terror, jammed in the car with the horn going, and this ruddy great pig sitting in his lap like a ten ton truck. The thief said he only wanted to eat a Mars Bar and this thing came over the back like a bat out of hell – or rather a pig out of hell. Clever pig, that one. Could do with him in the force.'

'Her,' muttered Mum weakly.

'You can come and get her and the car any time you like.'

Mum, Saffron and Duane went over to the police station. The car was outside. 'Where's Mona?' asked Mum.

'She's in the cells,' said the policeman. 'Didn't know where else to put her. Took four of us to rugby tackle her to get her in mind you.'

Mum looked at him with pleading eyes. 'You couldn't just keep her there? Could you? Just for three more days?'

'This is a police station not a farm, madam,' replied the policeman sternly.

'Yes. Oh well. It was just a thought,' said Mum wearily. 'I think we're going to need some more Mars Bars, I'm down to the last!'

They went down to the cells. The policeman got out his big bunch of keys and opened the cell door.

Mum waved her last Mars Bar.

'Come on out, Mona Lisa. You're free to go,' said the policeman.

Mona looked up and smiled.

Badger

by
Ted Hughes

The Badger in the spinney is the true
   king of this land.
All creatures are his tenants, though not
   all understand.

Didicoi red and roe-deer, gypsy foxes,
   romany otters –
They squabble about their boundaries,
   but all of them are squatters.

Even the grandest farm-house, what is it
   but a camp
In the land where the singing Badger
   walks the woods with his hooded
   lamp?

A farmer's but a blowing seed with a
flower of crops and herds.
His tractors and his combines are as
airy as his words.

Ted Hughes

But the Badger's fort was dug when
    the whole land was one oak.
His face is his ancient coat of arms,
    and he wears the same grey cloak

As if time had not passed at all, as if
    there were no such thing,
As if there were only the one night-
    kingdom and its Badger King.